The Salvation

Leah James

Copyright © 2024 by Leah James

All rights reserved.

No portion of this book may be reproduced in any form without written permission from the publisher or author, except as permitted by U.S. copyright law.

Contents

1. {Chapter 1} The hunt — 1
2. {Chapter 2} Alliance — 4
3. {Chapter 3} White butterfly — 8
4. {Chapter 4} Photo frame — 13
5. {Chapter 5} A mysterious person — 20
6. {Chapter 6} Picnic — 26
7. {Chapter 7} A joke — 36
8. {Chapter 8} Visitors — 46
9. Story on pause — 53
10. {Chapter 9} Grey — 54
11. {Chapter 10} Work — 62
12. {Chapter 11} Hybrid — 66
13. {Chapter 12} Helpless romantic — 74
14. {Chapter 13}Dead man's alley — 80
15. {Chapter 14}No way in forever — 85

{Chapter 1} The hunt

It has been 7 years since werewolves took over the world. At first it was a small part but they rapidly took over everything thing. Slaughtering man,woman,old,young. All except children. I don't know why but I have to be grateful otherwise I wouldn't be alive right now.

"LUCAS!!!WHERE THE FUCK ARE YOU? GET YOUR LAZY ASS IN HERE! NOW!" I hear my older sister shout."Coming..." I groaned as I got out of bed, already missing the comfort it brought me. I don't bother changing clothes and head over to the living room where I see my older brother and sister. My sister, Lucinda,Lucy for short,was standing with her hands on her hips while my brother,Lucifer was sitting on the sofa snickering. My sister was a very chill person so for her to get mad I must have done something stupid.

"Heyyyyyy" I start smiling,hoping to lessen her wrath. "Sooo what did I miss?" I ask. She groans in annoyance. "You idiot! Did you forget about the defence conference! Oh wait sorry let me rephrase that, You FORGOT about the defence conference! Now get your ass moving! You have got to be there!"

My eyes widden in suprise. She was right I had forgotten! How did I forget about something so important?!? The defence conference is held once in 3 months to make future plans about how to defend our safe haven from werewolves. I am one of the soldiers who is supposed to stand guard there as many werewolves try to break in.

"SHIT! I FORGOT!" I say as I move to the door and try to put my shoes on. It was 4:45,the meeting was going to start at 5. Since our apartment was close by to our main headquarters,if I ran I'd be there in 10 minutes.

"You dimwit" my older brother snickered. I glare at him before running out the door. If I end up being late, captain is going to kill me.

I reach the headquarters at 4:55. I see Aiden, my best bud at the gate. "Lucas! Thank god you came! I thought you weren't coming! The captain said that the conference will be delayed by 15 minutes and whoever doesn't get here within that time will be fed to he wolves!" He said chuckling at the last bit.

"Thank god. I forgot about the conference and slept in. Also I highly doubt that my sister will sit back and watch as captain tries feeding me to the wolves." I said as we both walked into the building. "True. Captain Lucinda would kill captain G before he could even lay a finger on you." He told me. I nod. My older siblings,even though don't show it,are as overprotective of me as any other pair of siblings. A bit more because of the fact that we are the only family we have.

By the time it's 5. Captain George,or captain G for short saw us. " Lucas, Aiden. You both are stationed at the opposite building's rooftop. It has a clear view of the conference room meaning you should be able to see the entire surroundings. I want you guys to report any activity, suspicious or not to me."We both nod and captain leaves us both.

We head on over to the building's rooftop. By the time we reach our place of station we stop talking as part of muscle memory from our time training. At exactly 5:15 the conference begins and me and Aiden report all activity we see.

At quater to 6, we see a black car pull near the building. A claw mark on the front door. It only meant one thing. Werewolves. I immediately tell Captain G about what we saw. "Yes I know. The president wanted to have a talk with the werewolves. I stood and still stand against it but I have no say in the matter." He tells us.

A figure comes out of the car. A tall boy probably 18 with dark hair contradictory to my own blonde hair. I couldn't see what colour his eyes were from where I was. But I knew one thing. His eyes were probably just a beautiful as he was. I couldn't believe it. While most people thought only werewolves could have mates it was not true. Humans as well could have mates. The only difference being that humans' weren't as sensitive towards mates as werewolves if you get that. But we could still sense whether a person was our mate. And I knew the moment I set my eyes on that werewolf that we were mates. I felt all my resentment for werewolves disappear for a moment as I saw him. But it came back, thankfully.

What do I tell Aiden? What do I tell my siblings? And what do I do? A werewolf and I for God's sake are mates!

What do I seriously do?

{Chapter 2} Alliance

I am lost in a tornado of thoughts when I feel a hand on the collar of my shirt. The hand pulls me down and I hit the floor of the roof with a thud."Dude!what the hell?!"Aiden whisper shouts at me. "I told you to get down!" "Sorry!" I say."what did you say earlier I didn't hear."

Aiden sighs and tells me that captain g told us to get down and out of there. We both make our way out of there."What do you think happened?" I ask Aiden. "I don't know." Aiden says with a sigh. He hated not knowing about things." Do you- do you think that Darius is going to make an alliance with werewolves?..." I choke out. Aiden looks at me widdened eyes.

When werewolves took over,many humans made places to stay and be protected from werewolves. But recently some of these places started making alliances with werewolves to have a bit for mobility and less worry about being attacked by werewolves. Werewolves started living with humans in places that were once there to protect us from those monsters.

"No." Aiden says. He would never be able to accept the fact that we have to live with werewolves.

Out of all the safe havens for humans, Darius is the one of the only places to yet make an alliance with werewolves. The reason being that everyone who lives here has a passionate hatred towards werewolves. Some people lost their homes, some their family and some their loved ones to those damned beasts. We all may have different reasons for being here but we all have one thing in common.

Hatred for werewolves. And that wasn't going to change.

I say bye to Aiden and head home wondering about what I tell my siblings. I reach home when I see my sister sitting in the kitchen with her elbows on the island in the middle.

"Lucas, you're here. Come sit down. Lucifer! Come here please." She says. She had a serious expression on her face instead of her usual stone cold face. I was worried.

Lucifer soon enters the kitchen and sits on a stool. I follow and sit down as well. "What happened is everything ok?" I ask immediately. Lucifer as looks at her with worry in his eyes.

"All though I am not sure whether this is true or not, I think we are going to form an alliance with the werewolves. I heard that the soon to be alpha came by to have a meeting with the president." She finishes.

Lucifer faces first turns shocked and then it turns to one of anger. I myself feel perplexed."what?" Lucifer asks. "Many of the captains are against this decision, myself included, but we have no say in the matter." She says. Just like what captain G told me and Aiden. "Although it is just a rumour." Lucy tells us.

"If it is true we have to leave." Lucifer says. Me and Lucy nod in agreement. "I think we should wait until the decision is finalised. It we'll be difficult to move immediately. The safe haven of Xers is the closest place near us which hasn't formed an alliance with werewolves." Lucy adds." And it will take us a week to reach Xers. We shouldn't make hasty decisions." I say. Both of them nod." Well that's all I had to say." Lucy says. Lucifer hums. Just as they are about to get up I say, " wait. I have to tell you guys something."

Lucy and Lucifer look at me and sit down. I know that I probably shouldn't tell them about the fact that my mate is a werewolf but I never have lied to them and i never will. I can't. I know they will figure out that I am lieing either way. And something stops me from lieing to them.

I take in a deep breath and begin" I saw my mate and... He is a werewolf." Both my siblings' eyes widen in shock. They look at eachother and then to me. After a few minutes of silence, my brother finally says "Ok." in a small voice. My sister nods. I know they want to tell me that I shouldn't think to much about it and reject him since humans won't die without their mates, they also know that I have been waiting for my mate for a long time. I have always told them that I would find my mate one day and finally settle somewhere and live happily.

" Anyone in the mood for pizza? I can make some." My sister says trying to fill in the silence. Me and my brother nod and she gets up to start cooking. Sometime after me and brother join her. The rest of the night goes as every other night for us and soon we go to sleep.

As I lie awake in bed. I think about my mate. Whether I can forgive him or if he is not like the other werewolves and doesn't want to harm other humans. I hope he doesn't hate humans, because as much as I hate werewolves,I have really looked forward to meeting my other half. I was willing to keep our differences aside for sometime and talk things out. If he was like the other wolfs and hated humans, I would cut things of. If he wasn't, then I would do all that I could to keep him with me. I would do whatever I could to make my siblings accept him.

As I lie awake looking at the ceiling of my room. I subconsciously touch my lips and wonder to myself about my mate. I wonder what his name is. What colour his eyes are. Does he have any family members. Siblings. What he likes to eat. How tall he is. My mind filled with thoughts about him. Then suddenly I wonder if I stopped hating werewolves so I think about one and my blood starts boiling. So I haven't stopped hating werewolves just because my mate is one. That's good news!

Soon I let the comfort of my bed engulf me and fall asleep.

{Chapter 3} White butterfly

Image of Lucas :>(or what I think he looks likes)[soo after reading the previous chapter i realised that I didn't explain the humans having mates things very well. But I'll try too in the upcoming chapters! Or have an entire chapter just dedicated to it!Alsoo to the small amount of people who read my brain rot story I hope you guys can vote it would mean a lot to me! Anyways on with the chapter!]

I wake up at 6 like every other morning. I go to the living room to see my brother washing the dishes.

"Morning!" I say as I go to brush my teeth. "Good morning Lucas." My brother replies. I know he has a smile on his face even if I can't see it.

"Lucy is out of the house and won't be back untill 8 at night. I don't know what happened all I know is the phone was ringing at 4 in the morning and all the captains had to immediately report to the HQ. Hell she even put on her uniform! It must be really important." He informs me. I peek into the living room with suprise. Lucy hates wearing her uniform.

"Mhmmmm..." I strech out skeptically causing my brother to laugh. "Sit down and eat breakfast idiot." He tells me. I nod and sit down to eat. I don't like listening to people give me orders but if it has something to do with food i will never say no.

I stuff my face with the pancakes my brother made."Delicious" I say before taking another bite. My brother looks at me with amused eyes. "What?" I ask him. "I thought you said my cooking sucked?" He tells me. "It does. But nobody can make pancakes wrong." I tell him. He scoffs and goes back to doing the dishes.

By the time I'm finished eating,my brother is already gone to sleep. I wash my plate before taking a bath and changing into a pair of greysweat pants and a full sleeved black coloured t-shirt with a white butterfly in the middle. I wear a pair of white sneakers before heading out the door and make my way to the HQ.

I reach by 6:30,not a minute late might I add,and enter the building.

I see Aiden and go to greet him. "Morning Aiden" i say as I sneak up behind him a thrown my hand over his shoulder. "Oh!Good morning bro!" Aiden replies in his always energetic voice." What's the schedule for today?" I ask him as we make our way to the center of HQ. " The higher ups said that we are going to recieve some training today." Aiden tells me. I look at him uncertainly. " Training? Are you sure? We literally completed our training by the time we were 16 and have been going on missions since then. What training could they give us now?" I ask him. "I don't know man. I asked the same thing to captain G and he told me to just wait and see." He tells me with a frown. I sigh and continue our walk.

We reach the center after sometime where we see Shea and Shulli,two other friends of ours. "Hey guys!" Shulli says as soon as she sees us." Brooooo. Shea and Shulli look so pretty today-" "with their dark chocolate skin? curly black hair? Shea with her blue eyes and Shulli with her amber ones?" I complete for him. Aiden has a thing for the pair of twins. His face turns red as he looks away from me. I had heard him say it many times over the years I have known him, and when I tell you that I am annoyed,it is an understatement.I shake my head as we walk over to the twins.

We all chat for a while before leaving. While me and Aiden had completed our training courses as fast as we could to kill werewolves, Shea and Shulli took their time, meaning they where still going through their training but they would officially be able to join us by next week. Needless to say, Aiden was ecstatic.

We head on over to the auditorium where there were already a bunch of people seated. Me and Aiden took a seat near the edge of the row two seats behind the middle seat. And soon what ever training they wanted us to do began.

Captain Michael entered the stage of the auditorium and began "soldiers,many of you assembled here have already completed your trainings so you all must be wondering why we have gathered you here. The training you guys will be receiving is not one to harm werewolves but this time to protect them."

Everyone goes quiet and soon a roar of anger erupts from the crowd. While Aiden was shouting with the others i sat in my seat in shock. I slowly looked towards the other captains standing at the back of the stage and saw my sister. She was biting down on her lip as if to suppress a scream. When she caught my eyes she quickly looked away while I continued to look at her, when she looked back at me all I could see in her eyes were so many emotions that even i couldn't begin to comprehend. There seemed to be so much frustration,anger, disappointment behind her brown eyes, yet somewhere I know I saw a glimmer of peace in them, as if somewhat happy to finally try and end the war.

"SILENCE!" captain Michael shouted, quieting everyone down. He went on to explain why we had to explain protect our enemies. Apparently the soon to be alpha was coming by to try and strike up a deal. Since there was going to be many attacks from neighbouring safe havens, we had to stand on guard because making the soon to be alpha mad would only cause harm to us. I only payed attentionto half of captain Michael's explanation. I knew Lucy would tell me about it as soon as we got out. I was still unable to comprehend what was said.

We had to protect werewolves? The same werewolves who killed our people? The werewolves who wanted to kill us? The savages who rip of our heads and display it like trophys outside of their cities? Those werewolves?

I am certain captain Michael did a good job explaining what we had to do because even Aiden listened.

Soon we were dispersed. As me and Aiden stepped I told him that I was going somewhere and that I will catch up with him later. By the look in his eyes I could tell he knew I was going to go see my sister so he just nodded, gave me a small smile, waved and left.

I walked from the auditorium to the the stairs. The captains' office's were on the 3rd floor but before I could even begin my climb up the stairs I voice called out to me," Lucas!" I recognised it immediately and turned around seeing my sister. She grabbed me by the shoulders and pulled me into a hug. I squeezed her back in return before asking her, "Why?"

She looked at me with the same eyes filled with emotions. "We have to Lucas. If someone attacks while the werewolves are here, they will definitely get mad and end up destroying Darius." She told me, her hands till on my shoulders. I nodded with my lips in a tight line. She smiled. Happy to know I understood. " You better get going your training is going to start in half an hour." She said. She gave my shoulders a small squeeze before giving a small push to get me going to the training grounds. We would have training for 2 weeks.

My lips were till in a tight line. I tried hiding whatever emotion that was behind my eyes.

She didn't answer my question.

{Chapter 4} Photo frame

We trained for 13 days straight, the HQ gave us 1 day to rest. Tomorrow the werewolves were going to come.

"Lucy! Lucas! time to get up! Have breakfast!" Lucifer called out. I got out of my bed and went to the kitchen. "Why are you cooking? Lucy usually cooks breakfast." was the first thing that came out of my mouth. "I will cook whenever I please, problem?" he told me. I shook my head and sat down at the island. Lucifer looked at me "Aren't you going to brush your teeth?" he asked with his eyebrows raised. "Nah, I'll brush after eating," I told him. He looked at me with disgust and said, "You are nasty." and went back to cooking. I did not care about what he thought.

"Morning," Lucy said as they entered the kitchen. Lucifer was laying down the food on the table.

"Morning," Me and Lucifer said. Me and Lucy didn't talk about the whole protecting werewolves thing after that day. She still hadn't answered my question.

She came and sat down beside me and soon Lucifer joined us too. We ate in silence.

"What are you guys going to do today? since you guys don't have training today." Lucifer asked. "I am going to the HQ to discuss our finalized plans for tomorrow," Lucy said. "Um- I think I will probably just train or hang out with Aiden and the others," I said as I took another bite of my pancake. Lucifer looked at us a little sad but gave a smile. He probably wanted to hang out with us. We hadn't spent much time together since me and Lucy are pretty much always busy.

I felt really bad.

We finished eating and Lucy went to change. I stayed back still sitting at the island with Lucifer. "Are you not going to go brush your teeth?" He asked me as he got up to clear the plates. "ya I am going to now... Hey, you wanna hang out this weekend? You know with me and Lucy? I'm pretty sure we both would be able to get at the very least one day off.." I said. He turned around with his face lit up. "Oh ya! I mean, if you guys are free I definitely would like that.." he said. I smiled and nodded and got up to leave and get ready.

As I was leaving the kitchen I saw a smile make its way up to Lucifer's face.

I go brush my teeth and get ready.

So, what do I do now?

Should I go training or hang out with my friends?

There seemed to be only one superior option considering the importance of what was going to happen tomorrow. So I chose the BEST option.

Sleep duh!

That didn't last long as I was woken by my sister.

She told me that I should do something other than sleep as she saw it as a waste of precious time. I had, sadly no other choice than to oblige to her orders and got up and decided to go training with Aiden and the twins. I gave them a call from the landline, which is a rotary phone. They were the only kind of phones used as we are in war and on the loosing side, so obviously we are broke. Anyways, they were free so we decided to meet up at the training fields. We trained for a few hours and discussed about the plan for tomorrow. It was mostly me and Aiden since the twins were not part of it.

We all said our goodbyes and left.

I reached home at 8:37. Lucy wasn't home yet.

Lucifer was sitting on the sofa reading an old book.

"Hey I am back," I said to announce my presence.

"Yes, I figured. You reek of sweat so it is difficult to not notice you. Go take a bath." He told me without even looking up from his book. I give him a glare and went to take a bath.

"When is Lucy going to be back?" I asked. "I'm not sure, she said she would try to be back by 10." I give a little nod and sit next to him.

"Hey Lucifer"

"Yes?"

"Why did you quit?"

"There needed to be someone at home to cook for you guys and clean the house. Did you think food was going to magically appear and the house would clean itself?"

"No but I could have easily stayed back and do all of that. There was no need for you to leave."

This had been bugging me since Lucifer left. He had no reason to leave yet he still did. I never understood why.

He sighed.

"I just didn't feel the need to work there anymore. Nothing was going to change if I stayed or not. Besides i prefer staying at home and you like fighting for Darius."

"I don't think that's the entire reason."

"It's not. But you wouldn't understand now. Maybe when you grow more mature, I will tell you."

I nodded.

He went back to reading his book.

I get up and go to my room.

I look at the photos kept on my nightstand. There were photos of me, Lucy and Lucifer. There were some photos of me Aiden and the twins. One photo of our family before the war. There was also and empty photo frame waiting to be filled. I would one day but I wonder who would be in that photo.

I go to sleep. It was going to be a long day tomorrow.

I dreamed of a pond or a lake. I was there with someone else but I didn't recognise them. We both were sitting at the edge in silence. But the silence wasn't awkward. It was comfortable.

Next morning

I had gotten up and went to the HQ after getting ready. I meet up with Aiden.

"I still can't believe we have to protect werewolves!" Aiden began.

I nod. "I can't believe it either. But it's just for today I guess." I reply.

"What are you going to do if Darius actually forms and alliance with werewolves?"

"Me and my siblings are probably going to go to another safe haven which has yet to form and alliance."

"Same! No way I would stay here if werewolves were also going to stay with us!"

"Well, let's just hope it's doesn't happen." I say wanting to close the topic.

Aiden nods and we just sit at the table doing our own work.

I was looking at some files while Aiden was looking at the list of werewolves who were going to come today.

They weren't going to arrive until around 8 pm.

"Broo! Look at this dude! Apparently he is going to be the future alpha of the werewolves!" Aiden said as he showed me the list.

At the top was a picture of a boy with dark brown hair reaching his shoulders and blue eyes. He had a lip ring and his bangs covered his eyes, not that much though.

"Are you serious?" I ask him. "He looks the same age as us!"

"He doesn't look the same age as us, he IS the same age as us! He is 18!" Aiden tells me.

I look at him with disbelief.

"Believe me if you want or not. You will see tonight." He tells me with a shrug.

I shake my head and go back to reading my files.

It's 8 before we know it. I was stationed at the same building as the one where I was for the defence conference. Aiden was stationed inside. I was the only one there on the roof.

By 8:10 the werewolves' cars entered Darius and stopped infront of HQ.

A black limousine with a claw mark on it's door was the first to stop. A tall figure exited the car.

I got a little bit closer to the railing to see if what Aiden said was true or not and sure enough he was correct.

I got a closer to get a better look at him and realised he was my mate.

Oh great! The future alpha of the wolfs is my mate!

I leaned over the railing a little more.

I wont deny it. I was curious and wanted to get just a little bit better look at him.

I probably should not have done that because the moment I did so he turned his head to look at me.

He probably realised his mate was nearby.

He looked at me and licked his lips at first before having his eyes widen.

He probably wasn't expecting a human mate any less than I was expecting a werewolf one.

We made eye contact and stared at eachother.

I wonder what he was thinking about. His blue eyes didn't seem to show any other emotion other than shock.

I stare at him a little longer before backing away from the railing.

His frowns a little bit but quickly looks away after probably realising what was going on.

Your mate was from the race your people had declared war against.

Things were about to get complicated for both of us.

I hope we both make it out unscathed.

I take out my walkie-talkie and tell my sister about what I just found out. She stayed silent for a long while before telling me that we would about this once we got home. I sighed as I cut our signal. I run my fingers through my hair.

Will he be the one whose photo I will put in my photo frame?

———————————————

{Chapter 5} A mysterious person

I focus on my duties. The werewolves were finally here and the president's decision would affect my life. So it was kinda important. No pressure or anything.

I kept watch for an hour which felt like an eternity.

No one tried to break in so that was a good sign.

No one on my side at least. I wasn't sure about what was happening near the borders. I just hoped everything would be alright.

As the meeting was going to wrap up, I saw a person approach the HQ.

They weren't from Darius. I knew everyone who lives here. That person was not one of them. They were also not part of the werewolves.

I immediately radio Captain G to inform him of the random person near the HQ. Whatever they were, they were advancing fast. Too fast to be human. And even faster when they saw me.

I don't know whether they were good or bad, but running at the sight of a guard does not make you seem innocent. Either way, they were almost halfway to HQ and started sprinting.

I inform Captain G of this and a few other guards nearby and soon enough some guards exit the building and capture the person. They struggle a bit and shout things I can't hear before being dragged away.

After the person is dragged away the werewolves exit with some of their and our guards. Aiden was leading them. The captains were standing around the future alpha. Xander if I remember correctly. My sister was standing right beside him. I wasn't exactly mad at that but I wasn't happy either.

My sister had no expression on her face as always. She didn't look my way which made me a little sad but the future alpha took a glance at me. I felt a little bit happy.

The werewolves got into their cars and left. The border would deal with them now.

So it just ended like that?

What now? Did the president agree with the alliance?

I sit down on the roof and stare down.

I remember the mysterious person who was heading towards HQ.

I thought about going to see what it was about.

Then I thought that I shouldn't do that since it wasn't relevant for me either way.

But I went to check it out since I was curious and I'm nosy as fuck.

I head down to the ground and start making my way to the cells.

I see Aiden standing near the underground entrance.

"Lucas? What are you doing here?" he asks when he sees me. "I wanted to see the person who was running towards HQ," I say. "Oh. Then he is over there." He says as he points towards the last room in the long hall which was the underground dungeon as we called it. It was the interrogation room.

"You didn't go over to the borders?" I asked him as I began to open the door. "No. Why would you think that?" He asks. "Because all the guards who were stationed inside were sent to the borders," I say. "Well, you are correct. I had to beg Captain Lucinda not to make me go." He says as we walk down the hall. "What? Sister has no reason to do that. She would not do that." My sister was a very strict person when it came to work. She would not let anyone change their duties or skip a day unless it was for a VERY good reason. "Well, it was thanks to you. When Captain G said that you would also accompany the werewolves to the borders Captain Lucinda immediately said 'No way. You are not sending my baby brother there.' everyone was surprised, to say the least. Since she excused you I begged her to excuse me as well. She was reluctant at first but she finally allowed me to skip it. I still don't get why she was against the idea of you going to the borders though." Aiden said.

Probably because my forever one is the future alpha of the werewolves. And a 20-minute walk with him was the last thing I needed. I have heard how werewolves quite literally kiss their mates the moment they meet them. I did not want that to happen. Although maybe the future alpha wasn't like that. Avoiding an awkward conversation was much appreciated. I definitely have to thank Lucy once I get home.

"She is just being protective of me. Besides I wouldn't want to walk with a bunch of werewolves either way." I say.

By the time our conversation ends, we reach the interrogation room.

"Sooo, what did you guys find out about this mysterious person?" I ask. "Nothing as of now. He won't speak up bout anything and has been sitting in the room looking like he is going to cry. He doesn't seem like a bad guy so we haven't forced him to say anything as of now but the werewolves will probably want answers from him and soon." Aiden fills me in. I look at him and ask "Why would the werewolves want to know what this dude said?" "I don't know. Maybe he is their enemy or something," he said with a shrug.

I sigh and enter the room.

A guy with white hair and sad blue eyes was sitting there.

He looked like he was on the verge of tears.

I go and sit at the table on the chair opposite of him.

I was a fairly friendly person so I'm sure I could get a little bit of information out of him.

"Hey," I said with a smile as I sat down.

He looks up at me. His eyes widen a little at seeing me.

Probably recognized me as the guard whom he ran away from.

He quickly looks down.

I sit there for half an hour trying to strike up a conversation and succeed.

After I figure out a little bit more about him I say bye and leave the room.

Aiden was standing there waiting for me.

"Hey, bro. So, find out anything new?" He asked me. I nodded and we began walking to the surface.

"Firstly, his name is Kyle. I didn't find out what he is. He came to see the future alpha and he is not on any side as of now," I fill him in. We reach the surface where I see my sister at the doors of HQ talking to Captain Kai. She saw me and waved. Me and Aiden walk over to her. By the time we reach her Captain Kai had already left.

"Hey Lucas, Aiden. Where did you guys go?" She asks as she ruffled my hair.

"We went to the underground dungeon. Lucas had a chat with the dude who was running towards HQ. Found out his name is Kyle and a few more things," Aiden told her.

"I see. Thanks, that saved us some trouble. Come on let's go home." She told us.

"You guys go ahead, I am going to meet up with the twins," Aiden said.

He waves at us and we wave back before heading home.

"Hey, thanks for not making me go to the border."

"I am sorry what was that?" she asked with a smirk "Could you repeat that? I didn't hear you"

"I said thank you dickhead. Gosh, you can be so annoying at times." I roll my eyes.

"That's my job as an older sister. Besides I didn't want you near the future alpha. What if he went crazy seeing you, his mate, and suddenly kisses you? I have heard werewolves usually end up fucking the first night they meet. I definitely did not want that to happen to you," she said as we continued waking.

"Can you take a holiday on the weekend? I want us to spend the day with Lucifer,"

"Ya, sure it's been a long time since we all hung out."

Soon we reach our house. I don't know if we will continue living here.

{Chapter 6} Picnic

We enter and the first thing Lucifer says to us is whether Darius is going to ally with the werewolves and if we will have to move to Xers.

Lucy and I tell him that we don't know and everyone will find out in 2 days.

We both go change as Lucifer prepares dinner and we plan on what we are going to do on the weekend.

And now it is time for the moment I dreaded. Telling my brother that my mate is the future alpha of the werewolves.

Lucy kept side eyeing me during dinner so it didn't take long for Lucifer to Speak up and ask what was wrong.

"So, I found out who my mate is," I start.

"Oh, so who is it?"

Great he doesn't sound enthusiastic. Well, I didn't expect him to sound happy, but with how he said it, I think he might flip the table when I tell him who it is.

When the werewolves attacked us, me and Lucy weren't nearby. Lucifer was. He was with our parents and he had to see them being ripped to shreds right in front of him. Me and Lucy only saw their dead bodies and the sight of the fields we used to live in being burned down. He had to see their lives fade from their eyes and be in the fire. We all had it hard but the trauma Lucifer got from that day hasn't left him. He once told me about how it was. He was waiting for us to come back as he sat with our parents and then suddenly werewolves barged in and started to strangle Mother. Father tried to stop them but he failed and the other werewolf attacked him. He was just 16. He could do nothing but sit there in shock as he saw the werewolves tear our parents' limbs and how they ripped out every muscle and every bit of skin on them, how he could see their insides, how a werewolf ate a part of Father's arm. He told me how he just felt numb. No anger, no sadness, just numbness. He wakes up still to this day due to nightmares plaguing his sleep.

And the fact that I thought that maybe things could work out between me and the future alpha just made me more guilty.

"It's the future alpha," I say in a small voice.

Lucifer doesn't say anything as if still trying to register what I said to him.

"Oh." That is all he says after 2 minutes of silence. The look on his face tells me that he still doesn't understand what I said to him.

"But-! I don't plan on meeting him! I don't want anything to do with him!" I say. I regret telling my siblings about this. I know maybe it would have been better if I never said anything to them and kept it all a secret but I have never lied to them. For the years we suffered it was better not to lie to each other. Keeping secrets would bring more harm.

My sister and brother both manage a nod and a small smile that doesn't reach their eyes. I had always told them about how I wished to meet my forever one more than anything and leave with them and go someplace far away. Away from the war. But it turns out they are the ones who helped start the war.

"Lucas, why don't you call HQ and tell them we both are taking the day off tomorrow? We all can go visit the little pond and have a small picnic," Lucy says.

I know she said that so I could leave the table.

I nod and get up and make my way to the phone where I dial HQ.

The conversation is short, they let me and Lucy have the leave.

I tell them on the phone. Lucy nods at me and both go back to discussing whatever they were talking about it. By the looks on their faces, I can tell it's a heavy topic and for some reason, I feel as if I am not welcome at the table so I just leave and go to my room and hide in my covers.

Today would be the last day I would ever see Xander.

I wonder what would happen to him.

While most werewolves at times go mad when they get rejected by their mates and die. I hope he doesn't die.

Well, I do hope he dies and I don't mind killing him. It's just I hope he dies from a stab to the heart favorably by my own blade but I don't want him to die because I indirectly reject him. I want his death to be more physical than emotional if you get what I mean.

I wonder if Darius really will form an alliance with the werewolves.

I wonder if we have to leave, how many werewolves will attack us on the way to Xers.

Will Xers also ally with the wolves?

Now, thinking of the idea of leaving makes me sad. 7 years I have spent here with friends. I have gotten to know everyone here. I have grown attached to this place. And the idea of leaving makes me feel sad. I never thought about it before but I don't want to leave Darius and leave all the memories we made here behind as if they don't exist. I don't want to leave. I will miss Darius.

But I can never tell that to my siblings. They are already hurt because of me. I won't do anything to hurt them anymore.

I shut my eyes and hope to fall asleep but I don't. The thought of the harm I caused to My siblings plagues my mind and I am unable to think about anything else. I think about how I am being a horrible brother to them by even wanting to stay here even if Darius does form an alliance with the werewolves. I still hate werewolves but I don't want to leave another home.

Now I am dreading about what is going to happen tomorrow.

We will sit having a picnic like what happened today didn't happen and pretend to be ok and that everything is alright.

I don't remember when I fell asleep.

I wake up at 6 like every other day and get ready. My siblings were probably already preparing to go outside by now.

I enter the kitchen where my sister and brother are arguing while packing the picnic basket.

"Lucifer I am telling you the blue blanket looks better!"

"Well I am telling you that it doesn't and we should stick with red the original one!"

"Whatever! What about the sandwiches?"

"I am making veggie sandwiches."

"Veggie? Are you serious? You should make ham and cheese! That tastes so much better!"

"OMG, will you shut up?!"

"NO!"

I just stand there watching them fight. They get so absorbed in their conversation that they don't even notice me take the picnic basket and fill it myself.

"Done. So are we leaving or are you guys going to bicker all day?" I said as I picked up the picnic basket.

They both look at me, then the basket in my hands, and then at each other.

"Oh- ya let's get going," Lucifer says and my sister nods in agreement.

"ha, you guys seriously act like little children" I sigh.

Now cue my brother putting me in a headlock and ruffling my hair and my sister scoffing.

We reach the field in a few minutes and set everything down.

The field is really close to the border so we set up our picnic close enough to the city that no werewolves will attack us but far away just as enough so we have a little privacy.

The picnic is actually really enjoyable and we just chat, make lame jokes and eat.

It was actually perfect.

"Then Aiden said 'that's why your dad's breathe smells so good'!" I continue telling them a story.

My brother laughs out loud while my sister has a little smirk on her face.

It was all going well until we heard some rustling from the bushes.

We look at the bushes as we begin to stand up and slowly retreat.

I was hoping that it was just a squad dispatched from HQ making their way back in but of course the universe had always been against me.

So the figure that emerged from the bushes was a werewolf.

The future alpha, Xander on top of that!

"Hey blondie! Ya you the shorter boy with brown hair! I am talking to you!" I shouted as he emerged from the bushes.

I was hoping he was referring to another dude who looked like me but we were the only people there so the only boy he could possibly be referring to would be me.

Of course I don't go "What are you talking about me? Wait I recognize you! You are my mate! But we can't....our love is forbidden.." instead me and my siblings make a dash for the city.

But werewolves being the supernatural fuckers they are, he catches up to us way to easily.

He reaches his hand out as if wanting to grab one of us and my heart sinks thinking that it would be my siblings. Even though they both were and are leaders for HQ I was still worried.

But he didn't grab them but me.

I felt relief for a moment but that turned into panic way to quickly.

Don't get me wrong I could take on a few regular werewolves on my own with out any weapons but he wasn't a regular werewolf. The was the future alpha so naturally he would be stronger, received extra training making him stronger and I heard a rumor that he was a blood wolf and he was stronger than any other werewolf.

Last one was just a rumor and I don't even know what a blood wolf is but it doesn't sound weak.

He wouldn't kill me right?

Ugh! Who am I kidding? I'd kill him in a heart beat if I wanted so why would he want to keep me alive?

"You shouldn't have tried running away" he said in my ear.

I hadn't really heard werewolves talk but his voice was so cold and deadly sounding that it was enough to send a shiver through my spine and making me static.

Is it me or does the field that looked green and luscious suddenly look dark?

And by the look on my siblings' faces I can tell that I wasn't the only one to hear his warning.

The first thing we are taught in HQ is that if a werewolf you know is stronger than you captures your comrade, run away and save yourself. So, according to that right now my siblings should be running away with their lives. But they didn't.

They were standing right where they were not moving.

I would be shouting telling them to run because I am the one the future alpha wants and I should be able to stall him long enough so that they could reach home and call HQ and if I was lucky have a limb retrieved but that wouldn't be fair.

Because if I was in their position I wouldn't move as well, I would try to protect them.

"What do you want from Lucas?" My brother speaks up. His voice filled with rage.

"Ohhh, so the blondie's name is Lucas. And to answer your question have a chat with him and then maybe kill him" Xander replied.

My sister reaches for her back pocket but before she can the future alpha speaks up,

"Put your hand down. I said I would maybe kill him. Unless you want him to die in front of your eyes?" He said as he positioned his mouth just 1 cm away from my neck. His canines brushing my neck.

My sister quickly put her hand back to her side. Her eyes filled with fury.

"Alright now let's talk." He said to me and in the blink of an eye him and I are standing near the bushes from where he emerged still facing my siblings.

He gives a wolfish grin to my siblings to show that I was ok while his hand which was originally holding on to my wrist made it's way to my waist and held on to it.

Now if you want to know how I was feeling, let me tell you it was horrible! Firstly I was scared to death yet still feeling I don't know something for him because of the mates issue and he was releasing his scent out to warn me and my siblings and let me tell you it made me feel scared, yet comforted but romantic as well but as if I would be killed if I made a wrong move. So in short I was feeling a whole bunch of things and emotions I wouldn't even begin to name.

So now out of my internal dialogue and to what was happening.

"I can't believe that a human is my mate." He sighed.

I really wanted to shout "You think I am happy my mate is a fucking werewolf?!" but I held my tongue because he was still really scary despite what I wanted to tell myself.

"Just so you know I don't want anything to do with you. It doesn't matter to me that you are my mate, I wont hesitate to kill you when I get the opportunity" he continued.

"Good. Now I won't feel bad about killing you."

Why did I say that? Why did I fucking say that?!

Ugh but in my defense he was getting really annoying acting as if I wanted this bullshit.

But I instantly regretted saying that because his canines immediately extended and were pushing against the skin of my neck.

"What?" he asked.

It didn't even sound that threating, almost as if he was just asking because he didn't comprehend what I said but again I was scared to death so I immediately replied with a,

"Nothing. I am sorry." in a weak voice, less than a whisper. But I am sure he heard what I said with his werewolf hearing.

And him smirking confirmed it.

Now I would never stand for this. In fact I would have started spewing shit the moment he caught me because I am a bit prideful but I had to think of my family. So I held my tongue for their sake and in the hopes that I could go back to them.

"Let's see" He replied'

His lips slightly brushed over my neck and before I knew it I was standing in front of siblings.

I turned to see whether he was still standing there and he took one last look at me before disappearing.

I had a feeling that won't be the last time I would see him.

Next thing I know my vision goes blurry then dark and I feel myself fall on the ground and faintly hear my sibling cry out my name.

That shit was way to much for me.

2452 word. I uploaded on time yay for me!!

Anyways, a sorry in advance if I don't post regularly. I started going to a new school after leaving the school were I used to go for 5 years and its been rough. I feel tired.

Anyways I hope you guys liked this chapter. I honestly want to rush this story up but writing this makes feel slightly connected to my old school so I want to keep it with me for as long as I can.

Please vote, comment if you want and definitely enjoy this story!

I am not that good of a writer and the fact that 101 people have read my story makes me feel so happy!

See you at the next chapter!

Byeeeeeeeeee!!!!!

{Chapter 7} A joke

I wake up in the HQ hospital.

My memory is a bit fuzzy but I still remember what happened.

That stupid son of a bitch. I swear I will kill him when I get the chance.

I look around and see the room is empty. That's strange why aren't my siblings here?

I see I'm still wearing my clothes from earlier.

While I feel disgusted because I reek I am grateful they didn't go changing my clothes. Like who would like to be naked infront a random people while your unconscious?

I look at my arms and legs to see if I gained any injury. Seeing as I didn't i touch my head as well.

Nothing there as well. I must have just passed out.

I would have gotten up and left but knowing how the nurses are, I stay in the bed.

THE SALVATION

It isn't uncommon for me to make trips to the hospital. Sometimes it's me and others a commrade.

I remember one time I got admitted and when I woke up I didn't see anyone so I just left.

When the nurses found out they gave me hell.

I think back to what happened at the field. How long has it been? A day? A few hours? I am not new to having been knocked out by werewolves but I usually regain consciousness by 2 hours but since it was the future alpha who knocked me out I must have been out longer.

But how long? Half a day or one full day? Or was it just by a few more hours?

I hear the room of the door opening.

I see my sister enter as she chatted with my brother.

"I hope he is ok. I swear I'll kill that mutt when I get the chance!"

"Count me in. No way he gets to leave like that after hurting our brother."

Lucifer and Lucy enter.

Lucy was holding a basket of cookies while Lucifer was holding blue hydrangeas.

"Hey why does it look like you guys came to attend my funeral??"I ask. I mean seriously! They were wearing black and had flowers as if I was dead and they came to pay their last respects.

"Lucas!" My brother said as he rushed over and hugged me.

"Oh thank god your awake!" My sister said as she came over as well.

"Hey don't ignore my question!" I reply still trapped in my brother's hug.

"The flowers are for the vase to make the room feel brighter when you wake up and the cookies if you were feeling hungry," she says as she picked up one and put it near my mouth.

I eat it as my brother goes one saying,

"You know how worried we were?! You were asleep for 3 days!"

"Hold up! Three days?!" I say as soon as I finish eating the cookies.

My siblings nod in unison.

"Then what about he announcement?!" Did Darius Ally with the werewolves?!

"It was delayed." Lucifer says."It's going to be announced in an hour actually."

"What?" I asked dumbly.

Did the future alpha delay the announcement because he knew I would be unconscious for 3 days?

Wait what am I thinking?!

"We don't know what happened but the werewolves said that the announcement would have to be delayed by 3 days because of some issues on their part." My sister said as she gave me the basket of cookies.

"When can I go home? And what happened to me? Like medically."

"You will be discharged the day after tomorrow. The doctor said that the future alpha did something to you so you passed out. They said they would keep you for an extra day after you woke up just to be sure." My brother said finally letting go of me.

"Dude why were you hugging me for so long," I asked him jokingly

"My younger brother was taken away by a dangerous if not the most dangerous werewolf and passed out when he returned you to us after he said that he might kill you. I have every right to hug you and be worried." My brother said putting his hands on his hips.

I put my hands up in surrender and keep the basket on my lap.

"How long can you guys stay?" I ask.

The staff of the hospital had a 8 hour visiting hour time and kept it very seriously. Even for family they made no exceptions.

"30 minutes. It's 11:00 right now." My sister says.

I nod. I wanted them to stay longer but I knew the staff wouldn't allow it.

So we just ended up talking to eachother for half an hour and ate the cookies.

At 11:30 my siblings got up to leave and said they would come by tomorrow as well.

Once they leave, I turn the TV on and flick through the channels until I reach the news broadcast.

There was a count down for when the announcement would air and the reporters where interviewing people.

I sat on my bed watching it until the announcement aired.

A lot of people where saying how they would leave if Darius did Ally with the werewolves some where saying how it might not be so bad.

They were interviewing the guards as well and I saw Aiden, Shea and Shulli on the TV.

They asked the guys some questions as well.

I wondered if I wasn't sitting here would I also be standing with them or would I be keeping an eye on things from above?

Soon it's 12:00 and it's time for the announcement to air.

My heart starts to beat faster.

What was the president going to say?

Now that I met the future alpha I wondered if he would Ally with Darius to just mess with me or he would intentionally make enemies with us just to make me suffer.

He wouldn't right? No way he would be that petty right? And I am just making myself seem way to important. No way my existence would change the decision he made.

The TV screen changes to the president.

"My people of Darius I want to being by saying that..... The future alph a's..." He takes a deep breath. "Mate is within Darius and because of them he wants to Ally with us. We didn't have room for negotiations as they said if we didn't Ally with them they would destroy Darius. So we have signed the treaty and from today onwards we are allies of the werewolves. The werewolves have also made us close the borders so his mate can't leave and so no other citizen can leave Darius. The border has officially been closed." He finished.

A reporter asked "Sir! Do you know who the future alpha's mate is? If so we can just kick them out!" The others agree with her.

"If I knew the identity of the mate, they would not be within the walls of Darius but the future alpha refused to disclose his mate's identity. He said that he would only tell us who his mate was when they themselves told us."

The reporters continue to ask a bunch of questions. But I turn the TV off before the president can answer. I just sit there not moving a single bone.

A nurse enters my room but I don't even bother to look at her. I try to understand what I just heard.

"Hey Lucas. Here some tea to help you sleep. I know how difficult this news must be for you. I know how much you despise werewolves." I hear her say as she puts down a tray of tea and some cookies of the table besides me.

I still don't look at her. I just continue to stare at the black TV screen.

The nurse leaves.

I understand what happened and pull up my knees and wrap my arms around them.

I wonder what Lucifer and Lucy's reaction was. Are they still watching the news?

What about my friends?

If they find out that I am the mate the president was talking about could I still call them my friends?

Everyone in Darius was probably hating on me without knowing it........

Is this some kind of sick joke?

Did the future alpha do this as a joke?

To ruin my life?

I know it was a direct attack for me because firstly the delay of the announcement and secondly the president specifically mentioning the future alpha's mate, me.

I can't believe it.

I knew he was a horrible person but I didn't except this much.

I never thought he would drag innocent people into our battle.

I can't believe I was this naive.

I look at the tray of tea and biscuits kept on the table along with the vase of hydrangea flowers and the basket.

I just want to sleep now.

I want to sleep and never wake up.

I take the cup of tea and drink it.

Do my siblings hate me know?

They went as far as to close the borders.

Does he want to trap me? Make me go insane?

He wants to make sure I can't leave.

But he knows I am part of the specialised unit.

The border closing only stops the regular citizens and soldiers from leaving. Not the specialised units.

What is he thinking?

Why is he doing this?

Why is he fucking acting like I wanted this?!

I didn't want this neither did he so why is he bothering me?!

Can't we end this on the battlefield?! Why does want to get involved in my life?!

Before I know it I finish the entire pot of tea and start crying.

I feel so frustrated.

I can't do anything.

I start feeling sleepy the tea must be doing it's work.

"Huh? Ugh. You really had to finish the entire pot? I wanted have a chat with you," I hear a familiar voice say.

"Xander,"

"Don't call me by my name. It makes me feel happy and I don't want to feel happy because of you"

I couldn't see him properly because my vision was getting blurry as my eye lids started to shut.

Now would be the perfect time to kill me.

I start falling backwards as he came closer to me but before I can fall on the bed a hand grabs my waist to keep me up right.

"How did you like my little gift dear mate? I changed my decision just for you."

So we were never meant to be allies it changed because he saw me and realised we were mates.

If I never leaned over the railing that day to get a better look at him this would never be happening. And he would have saw me on the battlefield.

"I have to go now so hurry up and tell me if you liked my gift"

I was sleepy and mad as fuck so I said the first thing that came to my mind.

"Fuck you Xander"

I don't know if I saw him smirk but I swear he was smiling.

He lets go of my waist and disappears as I drop on the bed. The tea was really getting to me.

I fall asleep in the matter of seconds.

I wake up at 10, far later than when I usually wake up.

I see a nurse taking out a BP machine.

"Morning I see you drank the entire pot of tea Claire brought for you last night." She said as she motioned me to sit up.

I do so and stick my arm out.

"I just wanted to escape somehow."

"I understand. The news was the last thing I expected. I hope that the werewolve's mate dies." She said as she started to take my BP.

I should have felt sad hearing that, but I said,

"Me too"

The nurse smiled at me.

"We will keep you here for today as well you can leave tomorrow."

Just as she is about to leave I ask her,

"Is anyone coming to visit me today?"

In this hospital if you want to visit a patient you have inform them prior otherwise you won't be let in. My siblings should have already applied for it last night.

"No, there were two people who were supposed to come today but they cancelled after the news was aired" the nurse said giving me a sympathetic smile.

I nod and she leaves.

I end up having some tears stream down my face.

I don't remember crying so much. I cried yesterday and today as well. But the thing is,

They hate me. Lucifer and Lucinda hate me now.

———————————

Hello! I forgot to upload the chapter yesterday so I'm so sorry!

I actually just finished writing it today. I haven't taken a bath in 2 days and am just generally feeling shitty so if I forget to update on some days please forgive me.

I hope you liked the chapter and I just want to say that the humans having mates thing I just like the werewolves' but less powerful? I guess it doesn't have as much of an effect on humans as it does on werewolves. Also 2120 words!!

Anyways that's all please vote comment if you want and enjoy!

Byee!!

{Chapter 8} Visitors

Lucinda and Lucifer hate me.

They hate me. My siblings hate me.

And It's all that werewolf's fault.

He did it to make me suffer.

If someone finds out that I'm his mate they will kill me.

I lived in Darius for almost 8 years I know how people operate here. They get a chance to harm the mutts and they will take it. It doesn't matter if someone dies in the process. I have seen it happen so many times. I tried to stop them but I couldn't. The people had been so broken that they became self-destructive. It stopped mattering to them about who got hurt after a while, Be it them or someone they never knew, they just wanted those mutts to feel just a bit of their pain. So when the mutts' future alpha's mate is right within their hands why wouldn't they take the chance? Everyone knows that werewolves' mates are important to them. They knew killing me would hurt the future alpha whether he cared for me or not.

And I don't even know whether my siblings would protect me.

I feel even worse than last night.

And to top it off I have a splitting headache.

I call for the nurse and ask her to bring me some tea to help me sleep.

"Heyyyyyy!!" I hear a familiar voice enter my room.

I stop my mopping and look towards the door.

"Aiden?" I asked with a small smile.

"Yup! It's your best buddy! Here to give you moral support while you stay at the hospital!" He entered and sat next to my bed. "what's up? You seem down." He asked worried.

"I just feel down.." I answer unsure of how I explain my feelings to him.

"Is it the news? Don't worry about that for now. You should focus on getting better." He told.

I smile looking away from him.

"I don't understand how you feel right now but I want to tell you that instead of worrying about something you can do nothing about now you should focus on what you CAN do. Right now the only thing you can do is get better. So focus on that!" He started telling me how to feel better about myself and other philosophical stuff trying to make me feel better.

I ended up bursting out laughing.

"Dude, how many self-care books did you read?" I asked.

"Hey! I'm trying to make you feel better!..... Also around 10?" He said as he broke out laughing as well.

"Where did you even find 10 books?"

"You'll be surprised by the amount of books Captain G has. And how many of those are self-care books." He said as our laughter quieted.

"I never knew Captain G had such a side to him. I always thought of him as a man who would punch away in the gym rather than read books on becoming a better person." I said to him.

"Captain G is a much softer person. I know for a fact he prefers to read than to train until he faints."

Aiden and I ended up talking for a while.

"Hey Aiden how did you get in?" I asked him when I realized that no one told me about his arrival.

"If you're wondering whether I got an appointment, then no I did not. I kinda just barged in after I learned that you were in the hospital. Although it was a battle I fought with the nurses to allow my entry I have arrived." He said as he twirled and made dramatic hand gestures.

I smile at the sight of my old buddy acting goofy again.

Since we started training for today Aiden stopped acting like himself. He who couldn't be serious for even a minute became an entirely different person in a week. He even distanced himself from us for a while.

"Mind telling me about the behind-the-scenes of the conference?" I asked unable to maintain my curiosity.

"Dude it was a nightmare! When we found out you wouldn't be able to be present for the conference the entire HQ turned upside down trying to find someone to replace you!" He started as he sat next to my bed again.

"Oh? Did they find a replacement for me?" I asked.

"Uh well no we didn't," He told me.

"Really? I don't think it would have been that hard to find a replacement for me?" I asked.

"You say that because you weren't there when the entire squad was panicking when we heard you wouldn't be present because you were in the hospital. Well at least the captains, me, and the others only found out after the conference." He told me.

I nod, encouraging him to continue.

"Ultimately, we had no one replace you because no one met the criteria. The twins and I were curious about why you weren't present when Captain Lucinda told us that you were in the hospital today and I left to come check up on you." He said and crossed his arms.

"And when was this?"

He checked his watch and replied.

"Hmm, 20 minutes ago."

I looked at him in awe.

I felt really happy inside knowing that my best friend risked everything and came running to see me when he learned I was in the hospital. I wondered if he would still see me and his closest friend if he knew who I was chained to.

There was a knock on the door as Aiden kept talking to me.

"Oh- Come in!"

"Lucas? The nurse said you would be in here." Another familiar voice.

"Captain G?" Me and Aiden had voiced out in unison.

"Hello, how are you feeling? Ah- Aiden?" He said as he walked into the room.

He was wearing his uniform. he had a scar on his left eye, already healing since it was made years ago but still there. He had his hair kept short and had broad shoulders with a strong build.

He was Aiden's role model and someone I looked up to.

Aiden almost passed out of joy when he learned we would be in his squad.

"Hello, Captain. What brings you here?" I asked with a smile.

"I came by to see how you were doing." He said and handed me a bouquet of peonies.

"Oh- Thank you!" I took the bouquet in my hands.

Captain G sat next to Aiden. "It seems your siblings have already visited you?" he said looking at the vase of hydrangeas.

"Yes, they came to visit last night."

Me and Captain were talking while Aiden was sitting there very silently.

"Aiden what's wrong? You seem quiet." I asked just to mess with him.

He glared at me. I could tell he was telling me that he was going to beat me up the moment I was discharged from the hospital.

Captain cleared his throat. "I think he is tired Lucas. After all, he must have used up all his energy when he ran away from training to come here." He said looking at Aiden.

"I- Uh- Captain-.... sorry?"

Captain G just sighed. "Well, I must leave now. Aiden I expect you to be present tomorrow and work overtime, just for today you will be allowed to stay and accompany Lucas. Take care." He said and left.

"Dude!- What the hell!! I almost got myself killed to check up on you and this is how I get repaid??!" He started whining like a 5-year-old.

"I was just messing with you." I chuckled. "I really do appreciate you risk losing your neck to come and visit me." I smiled at him.

"Ugh save it. I am so beating your ass once you get discharged."

Just as Aiden was about to continue on his rant I heard someone opening the door to my room. Me and Aiden looked towards the door.

Two familiar faces entered. No wait- Four people?

Shea and Shuli entered first and behind them... who was behind them?

"Lucas!" Shea said as she saw me.

"Uh- Hey Shea, Shuli. Who is that behind-"

My brother and sister entered.

They came? But the nurse said the two people who were supposed to visit canceled last night. If it wasn't them who canceled.. then who was it? And whoever it was, why would they cancel right after the conference? Unless they knew I was the future alpha's mate but if they knew why not tell the others? No point in keeping me alive. While I am generally kind to people I doubt anyone would keep me alive just because I was nice to them. So who were the two people? Could it be they are afraid of my siblings and don't want to risk getting on their bad side?

"Hey Lucas, how are you feeling?" My sister asked pulling me out of my thoughts.

"Oh- I'm feeling better," I told them and they all crowd around me.

They were all talking to each other and telling me how worried they were for me.

But I couldn't focus on what they were saying because, from the small gap in the door that my brother didn't close, I saw someone with long gray hair.

And I swear I swear on my dead mother's soul that they had wolf ears on top of their head.

1500 words.

Sorry for vanishing guys D: I spilled water on my laptop and it was out for weeks before I got it back, so I hope you guys can forgive me for not uploading for a while and missing 3 chapters :(

Since my summer vacas started Ill try and give you guys a triple update but that has to wait(im sorry T+T)

I hope you guys enjoyed the chapter!

Please vote, comment if you want and definitely enjoy the story!

Byeeeeeee!!!

Story on pause

I wanted to let you guys know that my house is being renovated and because of this the wifi is going to be out until the work is done

I won't be able to write and chapters for a long while but I hope to be able to start writing again by 10th of June or 15th June somewhere between that time.

I'll try to get a new chapter uploaded as soon as possible. Since my school is reopening I will be able to get my schedule on track again.

I am sorry for the 2nd delay and hope to be able to write for you all again as soon as I can.

—The Author

{Chapter 9} Grey

What was a werewolf doing here?

Something is not right.

I looked over at the others who were still chatting away with each other.

It looks like they didn't see the werewolf.

I should probably let them know about what I saw right?

But then again what if they allowed werewolves into the hospital because of the alliance?

But there is no way such a big thing would be approved in such a short time.

Then that could only mean that I am either seeing things or that werewolf snuck in. And as much as I want to believe the second option the first is probably correct.

I must be seeing things due to this whole werewolf thing.

It must be the stress that's making me see things.

I internally nod to myself, proud of my reasoning.

But-

What if I am not imagining things? What if a werewolf did sneak in? Then a lot of patients could be in danger...

I decided that it's probably better to ask the others about this and then decide what to do next.

"Um hey guys?" I speak up.

Oh my god, that sounded like a squeak. What is wrong with you Lucas?

They all stopped their chatter and looked towards me.

"Is something wrong do you need anything? Oh were we being too loud?" Shea asked me.

"What? Oh- no you guys weren't being too loud... I just wanted to know if the wolves were going to be allowed to enter areas like the hospital, HQ, and well any other place-" I say trying to make it sound as less suspicious as possible.

They all look at me for a moment then Lucy speaks up "Not yet. They plan on allowing it later but for now, the wolves aren't allowed to enter most places. The HQ and Hospital are especially restricted to them. They would probably be exiled from Darius if they are found inside here and HQ."

"Don't worry about this too much and just focus on getting better" Lucifer said as he boinked me in the head with a pen he kept in his pocket.

I roll my eyes at him and we all burst into laughter.

So, if that person is a werewolf they are not allowed in here. I wonder how I should find them.

I would tell my siblings about Xander entering my room but if I do there is a chance I might get killed by my people so I won't risk it for now.

First things first. Figure out if the person with grey hair is a werewolf or not. If they are what are they doing in the Hospital?

Time flew by as we were chatting and before I knew it, it was time for them to leave.

"Bye! Take care of yourself!"

"I'll see you at HQ bro!"

"We'll come pick you up tomorrow so rest properly."

I waved at them as they left.

It was late and time for the patients to retire for the night so not many nurses were out to make sure there wasn't much noise.

They may not be many nurses but they all are trained nurses incase some one attacks the hospital.

Now all I have to do is get out and find the wolf or human.

I really shouldn't my paranoia get the best of me but I cant help it.

I lay down and wait until my nurse comes in to tell me to retire for the night.

When she leaves the lights go out making the room pitch black.

I wait for bit until my eyes get adjusted to the darkness. Once they do, I get up and head out. If I get caught I will definitely be questioned and if I tell them I saw a werewolf the entire hospital will panic and I if I am wrong I will have to deal with serious repercussions so I have to be sure not to get caught.

I slowly walk down the hall.

This is such a stupid idea but I have to know.

The hospital rooms are separated between ordinary citizens and soldiers so I have to walk for a while until I reach the common waiting room.

Ok so I'm here but where do I start looking?

I look around for a clue or a sign to show me which direction I should head in.

Which way do I go?

At least there aren't any nurses here so I can look freely.

Wait- Why aren't there any nurses here? All the way from the hall till here there should have at least been three nurses but I didn't even see one, Where are they then?

What if a werewolf bribed them? But that isn't possible since the nurses are loyal. Then that means someone got rid of them. But who would be able to take them out? They are stronger than a regular werewolf. That means a stronger werewolf is here. But all the above average werewolves are under the future alpha. So he must have send one here. But why? If they get caught the treaty will be canceled, why would he risk that? He wouldn't. Every time the upper wolves have attacked us they have done it strategically which means this wasn't his doing. He wouldn't be this reckless. Then that means a higher wolf is acting independently.

I'll have to find that wolf before something really bad happens.

I look around and see a seat where the nurse usually sits. I approach it and see a baton.

I guess this will do.

I pick it up and Look around the chair to find some sort of clue. If all the nurses are captured we're in trouble. I have to do this quietly because if I wake the patients and they learn that the nurses are not here they will panic.

I notice a few strands of grey hair behind the chair. The wolf probably took the nurse from behind. And behind the chair is a hall that leads to the morgues.

I tighten my grip of the baton and head down the hall.

This is my best chance of finding that wolf.

I reach the end of the hall and see the door of the oldest morgue in the hospital. It was usually kept close but the door was open.

I slowly place a hand on the handle. With one hand on the door and the other holding a baton I slowly open the door.

The first thing I see is a girl with grey hair whistling while removing bloody gloves from her hand.

The second thing is the body on the slab.

They just looked like a mass of flesh. Deformed so badly that they didn't even seem human.

The wolf didn't seem to notice me and just continued to sing to herself.

I look at her physical form and the way she moves.

She is stronger than most werewolves but only by a bit. I could defeat her without many injuries.

I'll have to reveal myself.

"What are you doing here?" I spoke up coldly.

She turned around quickly, obviously startled to see me.

She looked at me with surprise and smelled the air?

"Woah you scared me! Don't just sneak up on people like that! Especially when you smell like him." She said in an annoyingly joyful tone.

She studied me and it seemed like she realized something by the way her tail and ears stiffened.

"I recognize you! Your one of the humans the other werewolves tell to be careful around! They all say your super strong!" She said stepping closer.

I didn't reply and just stood there.

"Oh~ to answer your question I'm here to find the alpha's mate!" She said.

I raise my eyebrow. Why was she here for me?

"I came to find his mate to kill her!~ She is only going to be hinderance to the alpha and us! I know you guys probably don't like her either so why don't you help me find her and get rid of her! I know you reallllyy hate werewolves and probably want to pluck my eyes out right now but even if everyone says you aren't someone to be messed with you're only a human in the end so don't forget I'm stronger than you and just cooperate with me ya? That and I'm here to find a wolf who is detained here-" The last thing she said got my attention. There weren't any detained werewolves here. The only possibility was Kyle.

"What detained werewolf?" Honestly she was getting on my nerves and I could kill her right now but I wanted to get some information.

"Ohhh you don't knoww. But you guys captured a werewolf the day the alpha came here and detained him. The alpha has been looking for him so I thought while I try to kill the alpha's mate I'd find that dude as well! Then

I'll be in good grace with the alpha and he might let me join his special force!"

"Special force? Aren't all werewolves above average under the alpha?" This was news to me. We all thought all the werewolves that could fight against us were under the future alpha.

"Hmm? No way silly! Only special wolves can join the alpha's special force! And only a select few are part of it! I won't tell who but I want-"

I hit her in the head with the baton and make her fall to her knees.

She looks up dazed. "How can you be so strong-"

I crush her head with my foot. I do it a few more times until more than half of her brain is smushed by my foot.

I learned all I need to know.

I walk over to the body on the slap. They were completely deformed.

Their face was completely skinned and their eye sockets were empty.

Their limbs were missing and what was left of the was bent and twisted.

Their stomach was cut open and most of their organs where outside their body.

All of their hair was gone.

Several parts of their skin was cut and the insides where burned. Their mouth was cut out.

I look around and see one eye on the floor.

I immediately recognize the nurse after seeing his eye.

It was nurse William. He was the only one in the hospital with those storm grey eyes.

I hear someone enter the morgue.

"Oh my god- Lucas? what happened? You weren't in your room!... Is that a werewolf?..."

I don't reply to any of her questions, instead all I say is,

"Nurse William is dead."

Hello everyone! And sorry for the long over due chapter!

My updates will be irregular but I'll try to stick to my schedule!

Butttt anywayss-

Salvation has over 500 views! It's near 800 views by the time I'm writing this and I'm so so so soooo greatful to everyone who has read this story!

I really hope you guys will stick around longer!

I hope you enjoyed the chapter and I'll see you at the next one!

Byeeeee!!!

{Chapter 10} Work

"Oh my god. That's Nurse William? What happened to him?" The nurse asked in surprise.

"A werewolf," I said pointing at the body of the wolf I just killed.

"A werewolf?" She walked into the room and toward the body of the grey-haired mutt.

"I'll explain later. Firstly call the HQ and inform them of this also inform Nurse William's family. Oh, ask HQ to send a clean-up team for the mutt." I said as I walked out.

Nurse William was one of the few people here to start a family.

Every time I ended up at the hospital he would take care of me most of the time so I had gotten familiar with him.

It kind of hurt seeing him like that.

Now how much should I tell HQ when they question me?

I am thinking of leaving the mate part out.

And I'll have to go question Kyle again.

I'll try and help Nurse William's family with the funeral arrangements as well.

Also, this should be enough to break the alliance as well right? Not only did a werewolf break into the hospital a restricted area for them, but they also killed a nurse.

I should inform Lucy and Lucifer about this as well right?

I leave the hospital and sit on a bench outside.

There was going to be a lot of chaos inside now, so I'd rather sit out here and enjoy my few moments of peace before I get drowned in work for the next few weeks.

I barely get 2 minutes of silence before I hear some cars pull up.

I see the president walk out of the car.

Oh the president came to check the situation out...

WAIT THE PRESIDENT CAME TO CHECK THE SITUTATION OUT?

And after the president, the future alpha got out as well.

What are those two doing here?!I guess this big but not so big that those two would come personally!

All that happened was a Nurse was killed by a werewolf and werewolves are not allowed in the hospital and that werewolf is also dead because I killed her- Which now thinking about it I probably should not have done...

And other Nurses could also possibly be dead-

Ok it's a big deal.

I really don't want to deal with this right now.

Can I saw I'm not feeling well or should I avoid those two altogether?

"What happened in there?" I look up to see the future alpha in front of me.

Oh- the future alpha Xander

...

The same Xander who was like 20 feet away from me?

"WAHH!" I scream startled.

"What? Why are you shouting?" He asked clearly surprised by my sudden out burst.

"DON'T FUCKING SNEAK UP ON ME LIKE THAT JEEZ!" I said my voice cracking a little.

"I didn't sneak up on you and it's your fault you didn't realize I was infront of you. Now tell me what happened." He dead panned.

The fuck?

God he is annoying.

"Sorry but I am a patient and you can't interrogate patients."

Lucky patients had a lot rights since everyone wanted to make sure the injured recover properly.

I leave before the the president comes any closer.

I'll deal with this later.

I hate working.

Hey guys so I know this chapter is way to short and badly written and I know I didn't upload for a week but I had my exams and I needed to study for that.

I also have a fever so I couldn't really write that much.

I'm really sorry for the inconvenience. I don't know how long I will be out of it so please be bit more patient with me!

again im really sorry!

{Chapter 11} Hybrid

I practically ran all the way home.

I'm pretty sure the future alpha tried to stop me but I was long gone.

The only reason I joined HQ was to fight werewolves not sit some where and do work.

I absolutely hated working.

Every time I tried to sit and do something even I know I can do I still can't do it and then I end up feeling bad about myself.

Which leads to me feeling even worse about myself.

I go from running to walking as I enter the neighborhood.

I reach my home to find it locked as it always is at this time of the night.

Well not always since Lucifer is home but due to the entire alliance issue even retired officers were called in to help. That's what he told me when he came to visit anyway

I reach in my pocket to unlock the door with my spare key only to discover or well realise that I am still wearing my hospital clothes and not my regular ones so-

I don't have my keys.

Perfect.

Aiden, Shea and Shuli won't be home either.

I can't go back to the hospital.

So I basically have no place to go to.

I mean I could go to the field.

But do I want to go there after what happened with the future alpha?

No absolutely not.

So where should I go?

Captain G's?

But he won't be home either.

How come all the people I know are officers or people working in HQ?

Oh my god am I really that anti-social?

But no I am friendly with everyone I meet!

But I haven't ever voluntarily talked to people…

Wait Lucas this is not the time to be thinking about your social life.

Should I just break into my house?

That seems like a good option.

But do I want to put in that MUCH effort into breaking into my own house?

No... Seems like to much work...

I'll just sit at the door and think about life until morning I guess.

Having made up my mind at last I sit on the steps that lead to the door of my house.

It was a clear sky so I could see quite a lot of stars.

How did my life turn out like this?

I sigh.

Until I was 10 my life was normal.

I had loving parents and siblings.

I didn't have friends and I didn't go to school since we lived in a somewhat remote area but I was happy.

My father taught me how to read and write and so much about the world.

I used to play with my siblings in the wheat field behind our house.

Then suddenly one day when me and my sister went out to gather some flowers, we came home to our parents dead and werewolves ripping them apart with our older brother sitting numb in a corner.

That was the day before their anniversary.

It would have been their 15 year anniversary.

After that 7 years somehow passed with all of us training to fight wolves.

My brother and sister became captions and I started my training to become an official soldier.

I finally became an official high ranking soldier part of a squad with my bestfriend and my brother retired.

Life was relatively quite and then suddenly I find out the person I am destined to be with is my enemy, the one I had been training to kill.

And within a few days my life turned around.

The safe haven me and my siblings came to live in decided to ally with the werewolves.

The day of the meeting I made eye contact with the future alpha and everything changed.

All my day dreams of falling in love shattered. And I became an unknown enemy of Darius.

I let out a another sigh.

Okay I don't want to do this anymore.

This is depressing.

Ah- I still have to talk to Kyle don't I?

But should I go right now? It's like 2 in the morning.

It's better than just sitting here and terrifying myself with my life either way.

I get up and start walking out of the neighborhood and to the underground dungeon.

Some things come to me.

In a few weeks my 18th birthday will be coming up.

This war will turn 8 years old in a few days as well.

I think the future alpha will also turn 18 soon?

Then he'll become the alpha of all the werewolves.

If he is going to turn 18 this year, he was also 10 when the war started.

Who started the war though and why?

I have a feeling 8 isn't going to be a lucky number for me.

I reach the underground dungeon and make my way to the entrance.

Will they even let me in? Seeing as I am still in my hospital clothes.

But to my suprise no one was there.

I opened the door and walked inside.

That's strange... How come no one is here? There are always guards stationed here... Did someone break in?...

I immediately grab the nearest thing I can find if I need to defend myself.

Which is a broom but it's better than not having anything to defend myself with.

I walk deeper into the white hall made of plain quartz. There was a simple arch over each of the 36 rooms. 18 rooms on each side.

After reaching the end I see a note on the wall.

"Out for a meeting if anyone comes in!   -The guards"

Looks they just went to a meeting.

I guess it is about the infiltration of the hospital...

I then go to the room Kyle is in. The dude who was running towards HQ when the werewolves came for the first time.

I open the door and walk in.

Kyle who I assume was sleeping suddenly woke up.

I smiled at him and said "Hey Kyle"

"Lucas-?" He seemed suprised to see me.

"Yup it's me I had a few questions I wanted to ask you-"

"Oh-" His voice was really quite, almost a whisper.

His white hair that fell just over his shoulders was flying every where.

I felt as though if I said even the slightest mean thing to him he might start crying his blue eyes out.

But despite his soft personality from afar he looked like a really sturdy man.

He is probably just a bit bigger than Aiden.

I got and sit at the table opposite to him.

"Is the future alpha looking for you? Is that why you came here? To seek shelter?" I asked in the most gentle voice I could manage. He definitely didn't come here for shelter, but I had to make it seem as if I thought he did. Then he might lower his guard around me. I observed his face to catch a reaction.

His eyes widened slight but then he gained his composure rather fast.

"Yes... Xander is looking for me... But not as in a whole manhunt kind of manner. If he finds me he'll be happy, if he doesn't it won't matter."

I looked him straight in the eyes to see if he was lieing or not.

He wasn't. He eyes didn't show any joy nor sorrow. No emotion. He just stated a simple fact. I knew from the look in his eyes there was no lie.

"I see... So you didn't come here for shelter then.. that's good" I said with smile as I place both my hands on the table and leaned in a little.

"Kyle are you a werewolf?" I looked at him innocently, trying to seem as a nice human being who was just curious.

He looked away from me. Just like he did the last time I asked him.

"Not exactly-"

Oh? He's talking. This is good progress.

"I'm a hybrid..." He replied looking down as if he was ashamed.

I wouldn't blame him. Hybrids weren't treated kindly. Most people thought of them as creatures who weren't meant to exist.

I don't make a comment for a while and wait until he looks me in the eye.

Then I give him a small smile and nod.

His eyes lighten up.

Looks like no one said many kind words to him for being a hybrid.

I knew that if I continued asking him more questions he would start crying so I just had a casual conversation with him for sometime before leaving.

I left the underground dungeon. And looked at a clock that was on one of the street lamps. It was 3 am right now.

I have a lot of time to kill...

Fuck it. I'll go to the field.

The sunrise looks beautiful from there and the future alpha wouldn't be around since he is probably attending the meeting.

With that I start walking towards the field.

Hello!! Your bitch is back and alive!! Had some serious motivation issues and my phone got fucked up but it's fixed now so I can still upload chapters so yay!! But my laptop is not okay and probably won't be fixed for a long time so nayyyy:(((

But anyways I'll see you all at the next chapter! Hope you guys liked this one! And with that.. byeee!!

{Chapter 12} Helpless romantic

It doesn't take long to reach the field.

It might have just been me but the grass looked more dull than usual.

As if the last of its life had been taken from it.

I went over and sat on the grass staring at the forest that was rather far away.

Perhaps I was staring at it to see if Xander would materialize again from there.

Or maybe it was because I had always been curious of what lied beyond those trees.

Although I was an official soldier i hadn't been beyond the woods.

And having lived here for almost 8 years, I grew curiosity towards it, the woods.

It was kind of like an unspoken rule not to go there but not like it was an official one.

And until today, I didn't have time to come here and actually look and think about them and not as just a fleeting thought .

There was nothing stopping me so why don't I just go and take a look?

But something felt forbidden about it.

Like, if I went in uninvited it would be rude.

I felt as if I needed to be invited to go there.

Is that why nobody has ever entered the woods?

I try and shake away my thoughts. I didn't want to think about anything right now.

I lay down on my back and look at the sky.

I couldn't see anything from here but if I was up at the willow tree I could definitely see the stars clearly.

What do I do now?

I can't even live my life the way I wanted because of the future alpha.

I will never be able to fall in love.

I let out a sigh.

"Lucas?" A familiar voice calls out.

I don't even need to look at the person to know who it is.

"Hey Aiden." I reply still looking at the sky.

"What are you doing here?" I could hear his footsteps on the grass. They were making a sort of crunchy noise. Just adding to the deadness of the grass.

He laid down beside me.

"Why are you looking at the stars from here? The willow tree is a much better place"

"I know" I reply. "But I didn't really come here to look at the stars. I was running away from the hospital and when I reached out house I realised I didn't have my keys and decided to come here."

"Why would run away from the hospital?!" He looks at me as if I was mad.

"Well I guess you didn't hear yet but a werewolf broke into the hospital and killed nurse William. Then I killed the wolf that killed him. And thennn the future alpha and president came to check out the situation and since I didn't want to be questioned I ran away."

"Oh damn Nurse William died? That's a shame."

"Ya it is. I feel bad for his family"

Aiden let out a 'mhmm'.

We just sat there in silence for a few minutes.

"What would you do if your fated one was a werewolf?" I blurted out.

I knew I was supposed to keep my entire ordeal a secret but Aiden's my bestfriend. I can't keep a secret from him and I wasn't going to tell him about the future Alpha and me, just try and get is opinion about it. I think.

"Well- I wouldn't be with them." He answered. Short and simple.

"Really? You wouldn't feel sad that your other half and you wouldn't be together?" I questioned tugging the grass.

"No, not really... I mean it would suck for the werewolf but us humans connection to our mates isn't even half as strong as those of wolves. I mean they could die out of rejection but us? We would love and we wouldn't even feel them that much." He replied still looking up.

"I guess-" I said, ensure of what to say.

"Look that's just me- I don't think you would be able to do the same thing as me. You have always been a helpless romantic and I know your dream is to find the one for you and settle with them somewhere far away from everything." He turned his head slightly towards me.

It was true.

I had always been a helpless romantic.

I always wanted to meet that person who would get me like no other.

The one I could spend the rest of my life bickering over small things but still loving eachother at the end of the day.

Someone who was mine.

Someone I could love as much as I wanted without worrying about them leaving me.

I always knew one day my only family -my siblings- would leave me and because of that I wanted someone I would never leave.

I wanted to know how it felt to see someone do something as simple as smile at you and still feel butterflies in your stomach.

Someone who I would love to do even the littlest things for.

Someone who I could bring flowers everyday.

Someone who would do the same for me.

Someone who would give me as much love as I give them.

Alot of people might not get it. Wanting a lover, I mean.

But for me it was a dream I really wanted to come to reality.

"Still-" I began "if my mate was a werewolf I would leave them."

"Sure~" Aiden teased.

"Also what are you doing here?" I asked realising that Aiden should be at the meeting they were holding.

"The president told me to go and find you and bring you back to question you about what happened." He said nonchalantly.

"Then don't you have to take me to HQ?" I asked chuckling a bit.

"Eh- when was I someone who followed orders? No way I'm gonna sell my bro out. Especially since he was admitted in the hospital but still decided to go and fight a werewolf with a fucking stick." He threw me a pointed look.

"A baton not a stick." I corrected.

He mumbled whatever and looked away from me and at the sky again.

We laid like that for some more time before I got up.

I reached me hand out to Aiden and pulled him up.

"We better get going- the president might dismiss you if you don't bring me to HQ" I began walking with him behind me.

"Don't really care- besides I know you wouldn't like that so I decided not to drag you over there." He said puffing his chest out.

He looked like a proud peacock.

It was funny as fuck-

As we continued walking I saw someone walking into the alley.

Our eyes meet for a second.

I would probably recognise those blue eyes anywhere.

The future alpha.

Xander.

{Chapter 13} Dead man's alley

The future alpha?

What was he doing?

Wait why do I even care?

"Isn't that the future alpha?" I could hear Aiden ask as he came up behind me.

"Ya it is... Isn't that the dead man's alley he is heading into?" I realised as I saw the star shaped mark visible from a bare wall leading into it.

The dead man's alley wasn't actually named so because people died there.

It was named that because the man who owned it died. Killed by a werewolf if I remember correctly. And since people didn't feel like making a cool name, they just called it the dead man's alley. Rather simple isn't it?

But it is like a black market actually. Parents tell their children that a ghost kills whoever enters that alley and people say many illegal things like human trafficking and selling of organs happen there so most people avoid it. And because of that illegal businesses occur there since most normal people don't go there.

Those two rumours are what keep eachother going.

If people stopped thinking bad shit happens there more people would start going there and because of that sooner or later all the illegal stuff would come to an end.

"Is he going there to buy someone or what?" Aiden joked.

"Who knows maybe he is going there to buy his mate or something"

"Maybe" Aiden shrugged.

All officers who work for HQ don't have right to meddle with safe haven affairs. We have a separate force for that. Which means we can't help with anything that goes on in that alley.

It's unfair but the common force does a good job at stopping human trafficking to occur in the alley.

But that's just on the surface, only insiders know how much escapes from the common force's eyes.

We continued walking to HQ. Aiden was infront of me now.

I looked back at the dead man's alley and thought about the future alpha.

I wasn't worried about him really, seeing as how he was easily able to hopitalize me. Instead I was hoping the people in there would do something to kill him.

Actually in that sense the dead man's alley was kind of an appropriate name wasn't it? Since people actually died in there?

"Lucas!" I looked at the dark brown haired boy. "Hurry up!" He shouted.

"Coming!" I replied and ran off to catch up with him.

Just as I was nearing Aiden I felt a shiver down my spine. As if someone was watching me.

I brushed the feeling off. I had a vague idea of who it was.

We reached HQ and pushed the doors open.

The girl at the front desk was pacing back and forth nervously.

We looked over when we entered and a look a relief washed over her.

"Oh my god! Thank goodness you both are here! No one in the meeting room is happy with the fact you both are so so so very late! Especially the president! He has been calling me all night to ask if you both arrived or not! And he seemed angrier each time!" She said, frantically push us into the elevator and sending us off.

"Woah- she seemed to be talking at 200 words per second" Aiden joked.

"Dude aren't you worried? The president seems reallyyy angry. What if he punishes you?" I asked him.

Despite what I said I wasn't worried and I'm sure neither was Aiden.

"Eh- you wouldn't let that happen" I told me.

"Well, we have a ton of experience with this stuff don't we?" I smiled remembering our times as trainees.

We had probably made every single captain in HQ want our heads at one point eventually. And it wasn't the first time we made the president mad. So what's there to worry about?

The most he would do is kick us out. And that would do more harm to Darius than to us.

For me it might actually kind of be a good thing. Since I could be away from the future alpha for a while. And me and Aiden could survive on our own.

If they did kick us out they would lose a lot of manpower. And would have to train atleast 10 men to elite level to make up for the both of us. And seeing that it takes atleast 3 years for a regular man to reach elite level they would bring us back.

The elevator doors opened and we stepped out.

The walked down the white hall way until we reached the end.

At the end there was a dark brown door with a golden coloured plaque on it which read 000.

Aiden opened the door and we both entered.

In the centre of the room was a rectangular table.

On the left side 5 people were sitting and on the right 5 people as well.

They were our 10 captains.

My sister was sitting on the left side.

And at the end of the table sat our president.

He was man whose age I actually didn't know.

Somewhere in his 60s I guess?

He had a set jaw and a beard.

His hair was black but it was now mostly covered in strokes of white like his beard.

He had a sour expression on his face.

Before me and Aiden could greet him he started "Soldiers why are you late? I thought I had made it clear that you must arrive as soon as possible. And Lucas why did you run away from the hospital?"

All eyes were on us now.

It wasn't new for me and Aiden to be here and for the president to address us with our first names instead of last.

We had caused a lot of trouble in our trainee days but after becoming official soldiers our trips here stopped.

"Sir, as per protocol I avoided werewolves as a werewolf had committed a murder." I reply and put my hands behind my back.

I could tell from the look the president was giving me that he did not buy it but moved on.

"Soldier Aiden why is it that it took you so much time to arrive here with Lucas?"

"Sir, I was unable to find Lucas for a large amount of time."

Wow is he not going to add anything else? He is bold.

The president looked like he wanted to shout at Aiden for the disrespect but simply frowned and shouted a "Dismissed!" At us.

We bowed and left.

And that was the end of that I guess.

{Chapter 14}No way in forever

Me and Aiden entered the elevator again to go down.

The moment the door closed Aiden burst out laughing.

"God- did you see the look on the president's face?" He said between laughs.

I rolled my eyes at him.

"Heyy don't act like you didn't find it funny~" he started poking me on my side.

I swat his hand away with a smile.

"Well just so you know Lucy is going to give me absolute hell when I get home."

"Oh~ that's true... Well it sucks to be the younger brother of the strictest captain."

The elevator doors opened as I punched him in the arm.

The receptionist saw us exiting and rushed over.

"Oh you guys are in one piece!" She seemed genuinely suprised at us leaving unscathed after disobeying the president's direct orders.

"Well not our first rodeo" Aiden replied cheerfully pating the lady on her shoulder.

That seemed to have made her even more perplexed.

"It's nothing really!" I told her slinging my arm over Aiden's shoulder. "He talks to much."

I flash one last smile at her before quickly walking away with the idiot I call my bestfriend.

I heard her say something about us stopping and what Aiden ment but that just made me walk even faster.

"Bro why are you taking us to the training grounds?" Aiden questioned. I soon realised myself that we were at the entrance of the training grounds.

"I don't really know but since we are here let's have a mock duel!" I said dragging him once again into the grounds.

"Are you sure? You are still in your hospital clothes," He chuckled.

He made a good point. Our uniforms by standard had high protection. It would be unfair for me-who is wearing just plain hospital clothes-to fight Aiden.

But did I care?

Nope!

It was just a mock duel. It was not like we were going to kill eachother or anything.

Just as I was about to reply to him I saw 2 figures standing in the center of the ground.

One was the future alpha. I could tell because of the hair and eyes.

The other was a dark haired woman with long hair. I couldn't make out her eyes from the distance I was at but I could tell she was a werewolf as well.

There is no way the future alpha was going to be around humans willingly.

Also the fact that the moment we stepped foot into the grounds they immediately looked at us tells me that the woman was also a werewolf because no human has such freaky senses.

"Oh- it's the future alpha and his right hand," I heard Aiden say.

"What's his right hand's name?" I asked him.

"Silena I think?"

"..."

"..."

"Let's leave,"

"You took the words right out of my mouth." Aiden said as he slung his hand around my shoulder this time and started walking away.

But before we could leave, we heard a female voice call out to us.

"You guys can train here, we are allies now, you don't have to leave because of us,"

It was the woman with dark hair.

Me and Aiden stopped at the same time and turned around.

I saw the future alpha staring at me.

It wasn't hostile nor friendly.

It was as if he was observing me.

"Oh no! It isn't like that, we just ended up walking here while leaving, we aren't doing any training or anything." Aiden replied puting his hands behind his back.

I nodded rather quickly in agreement.

"But the blond one asked you to a mock duel and you accepted. Is that not training?" She enquired as she walked closer to us.

Ugh the werewolves and their insane hearing.

She stopped 40-50?cm from us.

Her eyes were two different colours.

One was white and the other was green.

"The mock duel was just a suggestion, it wasn't anything serious. You guys can continue your training, we wouldn't want to disturb you," I quickly answered.

She seemed to have taken it as an answer and gave a small nod.

We gave a little bow and quickly left.

"Oh my god, that woman was tall," Aiden said.

"She really was," I agreed.

"Anyways, let's go home!" He grabbed my arm and we ran off to my house.

Aiden spent the night with us.

It wasn't unusual or anything, infact he spent more time at our house than his own.

We were all eating dinner when Lucy entered.

She threw her bag on the sofa and sat down with a 'thump'.

Lucifer glared at her, just as he was about to scold her for being messy she announced that us and the werewolves were going to have a joint training session tomorrow.

Aiden and I both groaned at that, but we went- although reluctantly - for training either way.

When we arrived, I saw a captain and Xander discussing something.

I didn't remember her name.

There were few captains names I remembered, my sister, captain G, captain Micheal and captain Kai.

We were told to draw lots to decide our partners.

Aiden drew a random dude named Johnson.

And just as my luck was, I drew the future alpha Xander!

We all got into positions.

I was studying him to try and distinguish my advantages and disadvantages.

He was a bit taller than me and had more muscle.

That meant I could move faster.

Well not really because werewolves were naturally stronger than humans.

...

I didn't really have that many advantages...

Oh well I'll make it work.

We soon started.

Aiden beat Johnson pretty quick.

Infact most of the people had completed their fights. Some humans won, some werewolves.

My fight with Xander was the longest.

He kept throwing punches at me and I kept taking them finding an opening.

I found one and closed in. I then hit his stomach with my knee using all the power I had.

That made me hold his stomach.

I used that opportunity to move in again and try hitting him in the face with my knee.

But he caught me this time.

He pushed me back and I fell on the ground.

He put his knees on my thighs and kept my hand locked above my head.

We were both panting alot.

He was panting less then me but I was proud I made him a little tired.

After a few seconds I realised how lewd the scene looked.

I was wearing short shorts and a white tshirt which was drenched in sweat making a bit of my torso visible.

Xander was wearing shorts as well but his reached a little above his knees. And he had no shirt on, so his abs were fully visible.

I also noticed a long scar on his abs.

I swear I wasn't staring at them, they just came into view!

Anyways practice ended after that.

"Hey come on let's go to the underground dungeon and try talking to Kyle again." I told Aiden as we were leaving HQ.

"And you want me to be there?" He asked confused.

I nodded.

"Alright if you say so..."

We went to the underground dungeon.

I tried talking to Kyle again, I didn't get much this time but him and Aiden got along well.

When I said I was leaving, Aiden said he was going to stay behind a bit longer.

"Suit yourself, see you tomorrow," I told him.

As I was walking out of the dungeon I saw the future alpha.

I eyed him up and down before walking past him.

"Are you only glancing at me now? No staring?" He said.

I stopped in my tracks. Did he catch me staring? I mean I wasn't staring! Not at all! Just appreciating some well built abs...

Lucas snap out of it! That is your enemy!

"What do you mean?" I replied calmly turning to look at him.

"I saw you staring at my abs, like what you saw?" He smirked.

"Ya, too bad your face, personality and literally everything ruined them." I told him tilting my head innocently.

"I know an activity where you could see them without everything you hate about me," I saw his eyes growing darker.

"Thanks but I would prefer an activity without you. You kinda ruin everything for me." I turned on my heel and left after that.

I could still feel his gaze on me.

...

Did he just flirt with me?...

...

There is no way I liked it.

Absolutely not!

There is no way I'm going to like that guy!

He is literally my, our, all of humans' enemy!

He is the reason my parents are dead!

Right?...

Well it might not be HIS fault for that but it's his choice to continue the war!

He is the one causing several of us to die everyday!

Unlike humans if he wanted he could stop the war all at once!

Unlike us he doesn't have a council which decides this stuff!

He is the sole ruler of werewolves, or is going to be soon...

Ugh just get him out of your head Lucas!

As I walked home, the moment when Xander said he knew an 'activity' came to mind.

I felt my face burn up, it was definitely from hate.

There is no way in forever that I'll like him!
